CAN I TELL YOU ABOUT BIPOLAR DISORDER?

also in the Can I tell you about...? series

Can I Tell You About Self-Harm?
A Guide for Friends, Family and Professionals
Pooky Knightsmith
Illustrated by Elise Evans
Foreword by Jonathan Singer
ISBN 978 1 78592 428 6
eISBN 978 1 78450 796 1

Can I tell you about Depression?
A guide for friends, family and professionals
Christopher Dowrick and Susan Martin
Illustrated by Mike Medaglia
ISBN 978 1 84905 563 5
eISBN 978 1 78450 003 0

Can I tell you about Anxiety?
A guide for friends, family and professionals
Lucy Willetts and Polly Waite
Illustrated by Kaiyee Tay
ISBN 978 1 84905 527 7
eISBN 978 0 85700 967 8

of related interest

Perry Panda
A Story about Parental Depression
Helen Bashford
Illustrated by Russell Scott Skinner
ISBN 978 1 78592 412 5
eISBN 978 1 78450 773 2

Not Today, Celeste!
A Dog's Tale about Her Human's Depression
Liza Stevens
ISBN 978 1 78592 008 0
eISBN 978 1 78450 247 8

CAN I TELL YOU ABOUT BIPOLAR DISORDER?

A guide for friends, family and professionals

SONIA MAINSTONE-COTTON
Illustrated by Jon Birch

Jessica Kingsley *Publishers*
London and Philadelphia

First published in 2018
by Jessica Kingsley Publishers
73 Collier Street
London N1 9BE, UK
and
400 Market Street, Suite 400
Philadelphia, PA 19106, USA

www.jkp.com

Library of Congress Cataloging in Publication Data
Names: Mainstone-Cotton, Sonia, author.
Title: Can I tell you about bipolar disorder? : a guide for friends, family and professionals / Sonia Mainstone-Cotton.
Description: London ; Philadelphia : Jessica Kingsley Publishers, 2018. |
Audience: Age 7+ | Includes bibliographical references.
Identifiers: LCCN 2017043228 | ISBN 9781785924705 (alk. paper)
Subjects: LCSH: Manic-depressive illness in children--Juvenile literature.
Classification: LCC RJ506.D4 M25 2018 | DDC 618.92/8527--dc23 LC record available at https://lccn.loc.gov/2017043228

British Library Cataloguing in Publication Data
A CIP catalogue record for this book is available from the British Library

ISBN 978 1 78592 470 5
eISBN 978 1 78450 854 8

Printed and bound in Great Britain

This book is dedicated to my mum.

Thanks to Alison, Judith, Sam,
Fred and Keith for your input.
Special thanks to Jonah, Nate,
Amy, Yasmin, Dan and Jake for
your brilliant reading and suggestions.

CONTENTS

INTRODUCTION

This book has been written to help children and adults gain a better understanding of Bipolar Disorder, which affects 2 per cent of the adult population in the UK.

- Children and young people can read about Bipolar and understand what it is and how it can sometimes be to live with someone with Bipolar. The book will help children and young people to understand that Bipolar is an illness and it is not something to be fearful about.

- The book can be read by children and young people themselves or alongside an adult. It is hoped that it will help children and young people and the adults in their lives to talk openly and ask questions about Bipolar.

- At the end of the book, there are details about organisations that support children, young people and families with Bipolar.

"Hello, my name is Josh, and this is my mum and dad."

"My name is Josh. I am 11 years old; I am in my last year of primary school. I live with my dad who works as a baker and my mum who works as a social worker. My dad has a mental illness called Bipolar Disorder.

Bipolar Disorder is an illness, which means sometimes my dad is well; he works, plays with me and we go out as a family. Other days, he can be extremely happy, this is called being in a manic episode, and some days he can be very depressed and sad.

Most of the time you wouldn't know my dad has an illness, as you cannot see it. But sometimes you might notice that things seem a bit different. Some days Dad seems overly excited, he talks quickly and likes to spend money and he finds it hard to sleep at night; this is when he is in a manic episode. Other days Dad doesn't want to do anything as he feels very sad and depressed.

Nobody really knows why people get Bipolar or what causes it; some researchers are looking at genetics and the biology of the brain to try to understand more about the illness. What is known is that you cannot catch Bipolar from other people, unlike when you have an illness such as flu. Knowing someone with Bipolar does not mean you will get it. It is not the person's fault they have Bipolar, it just happens.

Sometimes too much stress can act as a trigger to a Bipolar episode. This could be stress from lots of changes or Christmas or exams or moving house or meeting deadlines."

"You can't really see a mental illness."

"You can't see a mental illness; it isn't like having a broken leg or being in a wheelchair. It is still an illness, but one which affects the mind and sometimes how you think. Having a mental illness doesn't mean you are ill all of the time. Some days can be mixed, and sometimes you feel much better than other days. Sometimes Dad is well for over a year and other times he is ill for a few months. Most people with a mental illness can do all the normal things in life everyone else does, such as working, seeing friends and having a family.

Lots of people throughout history had a mental illness, but for many years people did not like to talk about it. They would use horrible words, sometimes describing people as mad; they thought that people with a mental illness couldn't work and could not be parents. When Dad first heard he had Bipolar someone at his work said he would never be able to work again, but they were wrong. Lots of people who have Bipolar and other mental illnesses work.

People understand mental illness a lot more these days. Lots of famous people have a mental illness and have started to talk about it. Some examples are:

- Justin Bieber – he is a singer and has talked about being depressed.
- Zoella – she is a vlogger and talks a lot about panic attacks and being depressed and anxious.
- Stephen Fry – he is an actor and writer who has Bipolar.
- Zayn Malik – he was in a band called One Direction and has talked about having extreme anxiety.
- Prince Harry – he has talked about being depressed and anxious due to grief after his mum's death."

"There are several different sorts of mental illness; Bipolar is one type. Bipolar is a mood disorder; it is thought to be caused by a mix of genetics and the environment. My dad found out he had Bipolar when he was 20. Bipolar affects both men and women of all ages and backgrounds.

Bipolar affects how you feel; because of this it is called a mood disorder. With Bipolar your mood changes from being very high (this is called a manic episode) to being extremely low (this is called depression). In between times, you can feel well.

Bipolar affects your energy levels: when people have a manic episode, they can have lots and lots of energy; when they have a low period, they can have very little energy and find it hard to do everyday things. When Dad has a manic episode, he has loads of energy, lots of new ideas and masses of enthusiasm for everything.

With Bipolar, the brain finds it difficult to control the ups and downs of a normal mood. Everyone has mood swings when sometimes they are happy and sometimes they are sad, but with Bipolar these are very severe mood swings, being extremely happy and desperately sad.

You can only be diagnosed with Bipolar by a doctor called a psychiatrist. They specialise in mental health. Dad saw his GP first, after he'd had a manic episode for a few weeks and felt very low. His friends were worried and told him to see the GP. The GP then referred him to a psychiatrist.

There are two types of Bipolar:[1]

Bipolar I – this is what my dad has. To be diagnosed with Bipolar I, the person will have experienced at least one period of a manic episode (extremely happy) which lasted longer than one week. They might also have had some times of being very depressed.

Bipolar II – to be diagnosed with Bipolar II, the person will have had at least one period of extreme depression and some days of mania.

Sometimes it can take a long time for people to be given a diagnosis of Bipolar."

---

1 www.mind.org.uk/information-support/types-of-mental-health-problems/bipolar-disorder/types-of-bipolar/#.Wabw7a2ZP3

"When Dad has a manic episode, he can do some strange things."

"One day I came home from school and Dad had packed all the suitcases and told me we were all going to Australia, he had bought the tickets, and we were getting the flight that night. When Mum came home, she was cross and reminded him they both had work that week and I had school, and we couldn't just go to Australia that night. This was a time when Dad had a manic episode; he thought flying to Australia would be an exciting adventure. Being impulsive is quite common when people have a manic episode.

Here are some common behaviours when a person is having a manic episode:

- Sleeping a lot less, sometimes not sleeping at all. Once Dad went three nights without any sleep.
- Being very active, organising lots of things, and having lots of energy.
- Being more sociable – they might arrange a party or invite lots of people to see them. Several times Dad has arranged a party during a mania time – inviting loads of people, some he didn't know.
- Feeling more irritable and grumpy.
- Being very chatty and talking quickly.

- Finding it hard to concentrate and being distracted very easily or having lots and lots of ideas whizzing through their mind. Dad once planned five big meals, a party, a new business idea and started to redesign the house and garden while he was having a manic time.

- Taking more risks.

- Being more impulsive, choosing to do things in the moment that they wouldn't usually do.

- Spending lots of money or buying things they would never normally buy. Dad once came home with a new bike for each of us; Mum made him take them all back.

Some people like being in a manic episode. They find it exhilarating and exciting; other people find these times frightening and feel out of control. Dad says he feels free and alive when he is in a manic time.

It can be worrying for family and friends when you can see a person with Bipolar having a manic episode. You learn to recognise the warning signs, and it can be concerning knowing they are becoming ill again.

When I see Dad is starting to behave in a manic way, I tell Mum about my concerns. Sometimes it is the small things that make me realise he is becoming ill; when he starts to buy things he would never normally buy at the supermarket, or when he starts to talk about redecorating the whole house and looks to buy lots of new items, then I know he is starting to get ill. The warning signs are different for everyone."

"After my dad has had a manic episode
he becomes very depressed."

"Everybody has days when they feel a bit sad. However, the depression after a manic episode is stronger than feeling a bit sad, and it can go on for days or weeks. Often after a manic episode my dad becomes very, very tired, and he needs to sleep a lot. This is partly because he has missed lots of sleep during his manic time, but also because being depressed makes him extremely tired. Dad collects me after school each day, and when he is having a low period he can find it very difficult to get out of the house to collect me.

Here are some common behaviours when a person is having a low episode:

- Having sleep problems – some people sleep loads, while others find it hard to sleep but feel very tired.

- Having low energy, finding it difficult to motivate themselves to do something, feeling sluggish and slow. When Dad is having a low period, he finds it hard to be motivated to cook tea; he normally loves cooking and does most of the cooking at home when he is well.

- Finding it difficult to enjoy things. Dad usually enjoys watching funny films with me but when he is having a low period he doesn't find them funny anymore.

- Not wanting to be with others – they often want to avoid people and instead be on their own.

- Thinking they are useless and feeling bad about themselves. Dad is a brilliant baker, he is very good at his job and makes the most amazing cakes, but when he is low, he feels his cakes are rubbish and he doesn't believe people want to eat them.

- Feeling very anxious – this anxiety can cause them to think of lots of terrible things that might happen. When Dad is having a low episode, he worries a lot about me; he thinks I will be run over by a car when I am walking to the shops and he doesn't like me riding my bike, as he thinks I will fall off and die.

- Feeling very sad and crying a lot – the smallest things can upset them, such as burning some toast.

- Being irritable and snappy. I worry it is my fault that Dad is cross, but Mum always tells me it is not my fault, it is the illness.

- Wanting to hurt themselves.

Often people who have Bipolar say the lows are utterly horrible and find them much harder than the manic times. Sometimes it feels as if the lows go on for ages and ages. The low times can make everyone around the person feel sad.

It can be hard for family and friends when people are having a low episode. The person with Bipolar can become quite isolated and not want to spend time with family and friends. It is sometimes difficult when they are extremely anxious and worried all the time. When someone with Bipolar is very low, this can affect their work."

"Dad's illness makes me feel sad."

"Sometimes Dad's illness makes me feel sad. I am not scared by his illness, but it makes me feel sad when I can see he is so unwell. Some of my friends think it is funny when he is in a manic episode because he can do funny things and he is very generous, but I find these times really hard because I know it means he is ill. I know that after the high he will become terribly low. Sometimes children can be mean about mental illness because they don't understand it; sometimes they say cruel things about mental illness.

It is hard when people you love are depressed and low. I try to be kind and I try to understand that Dad doesn't want to go out or cook with me, but sometimes I worry that he will stay depressed for a long, long time or that he will never want to cook with me again. It can be difficult when he is low because he can be a bit snappy and I need to be quieter in the house.

When Dad is low I usually make him a cake. He has taught me how to bake delicious cakes. I know the cakes he likes and I know that when I cook for him he feels loved. I always hope that making him a cake will make him smile and feel a little bit happier.

When I am feeling sad about Dad's illness I can talk to Mum. She explains to me every time that it is the illness that is making him low or high and that he loves me and will always love me. It helps to hear that again and again."

"I love baking with Dad."

"Dad is not ill all the time; he is well more than he is ill. When Dad is well we bake together. We usually do this once a week; it is a special me and Dad time. Dad has taught me how to bake the most amazing and tasty cakes. Dad says I am really good at baking; my friends are all impressed with my baking too.

Mum says I need to enjoy the times that Dad is well. I think she is right, and that is why baking together is so good, as we both enjoy it. When he is well it is easy to forget about his illness, but sometimes the thoughts of his illness creep in and I wonder when he will be ill again.

Dad says he enjoys baking with me and that when he is ill he tries to remember how we bake together, as that makes him feel happier. Dad reminds me again and again that he loves me, that the illness will never stop him loving me."

"Most people with Bipolar will have some medication to help them; it is important to take this every day and for the person to meet with their GP regularly to check how the medication is working. The medication can make people feel tired and forgetful, so it is good to talk about this with the GP. Sometimes Dad decides to stop taking the medication, as he hates taking it, but when that happens he starts to get unwell again.

Just like everyone else, it is really important that people with Bipolar:

- eat well – there are some types of food and drink that can help moods. Eating regularly and drinking enough water is important. Dad decided to stop drinking alcohol, as he found that was not helping his Bipolar. Each morning he drinks a smoothie to make sure he is getting enough fruit and vegetables every day

- have enough sleep and a good bedtime routine

- take exercise – this is good for mental health. It can be good for someone having a manic episode, as it uses up energy. It is also good when someone is feeling low, as it releases endorphins – these are feel-good chemicals in the brain that help us to feel happier. Dad started running two years ago; he runs every day and says it makes him feel really good

- spend time outside – new research has shown that this can be good for mental health, whether it is gardening or going for a walk in the woods or in a field. They call this ecotherapy. There are some groups people can join or they can just do it themselves

- have time that is quiet and peaceful. It is especially important that people with Bipolar get time for themselves – time that is quiet and relaxing. Some people find doing yoga and mindfulness really helpful

- have people they can talk to and be honest with about how they are feeling. Dad has two friends he can talk to; they used to go to school together. They are good at making sure they stay in touch with him when he is having a low episode and does not want to see people.

There are groups people with Bioplar can join, where they can meet with other people with the same illness and find out what helps them. There are also online support groups.

When someone is having a manic episode or a really low time, it is important to ask for help, go back to the GP and ask to see the psychiatrist again. In some areas there are community mental health teams who can help and support when people become very unwell. The GP can make a referral to the team.

Some people find it helpful to see a psychologist, a specially trained person who understands how the mind works and can talk and listen to them. The GP can make a referral to a psychologist."

"A few of my friends know about Dad's illness."

"My two closest friends know about Dad's illness. Mum and Dad have both told me that Bipolar is nothing to be ashamed of, it is an illness and people need to learn about it.

Mum says people never used to talk about mental illness. In my school, it is talked about. One boy in my class has anxiety and another girl's mum is often very depressed. The headteacher has done assemblies about mental illness. For a while, I was afraid that my friends would think my dad was weird because sometimes he is very happy and sometimes he is very sad, but my friends say they think Dad is cool, as he bakes such brilliant cakes – they all want him to make their birthday cakes!

I don't hide Dad's illness but I don't talk to everyone in my class about it. If I am worried that Dad is having a manic episode I can tell my two closest friends. I know they will try to understand. When Dad is having a low time, they invite me to their houses to watch funny films or to cook with them, as they know that makes me happy.

There is a teaching assistant in our school who I can talk to about Dad; she understands as her daughter has Bipolar. When I feel really sad and worried I go and find her and talk to her about it."

HOW FRIENDS CAN HELP

- Be there to listen to your friend. Don't be afraid to ask how their parent is and how they are.

- Remind them to talk to an adult they can trust. This might be a teacher or another adult in school. It is important that the adults in school know when a parent is ill.

- Be kind to your friend; it can be quite worrying when their parent is ill. Life at home might be stressful. They might be feeling stressed and a bit snappy or be a bit quiet, so be understanding about this.

- Be normal with your friend; they still want to have fun, play games and talk about the things you always talk about. Having a parent who is mentally ill does not change who they are.

HOW SCHOOL CAN HELP

- Make sure you have good communication with home. Encourage parents to update you when a parent is becoming ill – explain that this is about you being able to support the child.

- Ensure you have a named person for the child to talk to. This could be a teaching assistant or the special educational needs co-ordinator – someone who is consistent. It is often better to have someone different from the class teacher. Make sure this person checks in with the child to see how they are, especially when it is known that the parent is ill. Remind the child that the named person is there for them.

- With each new teacher, let them know about Bipolar. If they are not familiar with the illness, get them to read this book.

- During a transition to a new school, make sure you inform the new school about the Bipolar, and tell the family that you are doing this. This ensures that the new school understands what is happening for the child and family.

- Talk about mental health in school; make it known this is not a taboo subject.

- When a parent is ill, it can be very hard for the child to concentrate on school work. They may be easily distracted, falling out with friends, getting behind with work and not keeping up with homework. Ensure you are putting in support to look after the child's wellbeing. Remind the child that their parent loves them.

SERVICES THAT SUPPORT

Most local authorities have a young carers service, which is often run by a local charity. The child may find this a useful group, as it gives them the opportunity to talk to other children and young people who have family members with an illness. It can be a good support network for the child.

Mind is a national charity and it also has local branches. Each local branch will run different services, including support groups for people with mental health issues and for family members – www.mind.org.uk

Bipolar UK is a national charity. It has a website and a support line. There are also support groups across the UK – www.bipolaruk.org

YoungMinds is a charity for children and young people. It has lots of information about mental illness and runs support groups – https://youngminds.org.uk

Kidstime Foundation runs some groups across the country and has a website for children about parents' mental illness – http://kidstimefoundation.org

RECOMMENDED READING

BOOKS

Mummy's Got Bipolar by Sonia Mainstone-Cotton, published by Jonson. A picture book aimed at children aged three to seven years.

The Illustrated Mum by Jacqueline Wilson, published by Transworld. The mum in the story has Bipolar Disorder.

The Wise Mouse by Virginia Ironside, published by YoungMinds. The mum in the story has a mental illness.